UNIVERSAL PICTURES PRESENTS
AN ASPEN FILM SOCIETY WILLIAM E. McEUEN – DAVID V. PICKER PRODUCTION
A CARL REINER FILM

STEVE MARTIN

in

The JERK

also starring

BERNADETTE PETERS

CATLIN ADAMS

and JACKIE MASON as Harry Hartounian

Screenplay by

STEVE MARTIN, CARL GOTTLIEB, MICHAEL ELIAS

Story by

STEVE MARTIN and CARL GOTTLIEB

Produced by

DAVID V. PICKER and WILLIAM E. McEUEN

Directed by

CARL REINER

A UNIVERSAL PICTURE

The JERK

**Screenplay by Steve Martin,
Carl Gottlieb, Michael Elias**

Story by Steve Martin & Carl Gottlieb

**Introduction and text adaptation
by Carl Gottlieb**

Designed by Tom Nozkowski

WARNER BOOKS

A Warner Communications Company

INTRODUCTION

I was trekking in the Himalayas of Nepal in 1973, in the company of trader-adventurer Milan Melvin and an American named Addison Smith who had lived in Asia for seven years. On the night of my birthday there was a full moon; I lay in my sleeping bag in a remote unnamed village near the headwaters of the Buri Gandaki, a river to the west of Kathmandu. Four years later, almost to the day, Steve Martin and I completed the first draft of the screenplay of THE JERK. The two events were unrelated, and the movie includes nothing of my Himalayan experience.

BACKGROUND

Steve Martin and I first became acquainted in the summer of 1968, when we were among some new and untried talent hired to write the Smothers Brothers summer replacement show on the CBS network. I starred Glen Campbell, and that Autumn, us New Kids had our options picked up, and went to work writing the Smothers Brothers Comedy Hour, then in its third season on CBS. After a fuss over censorship, satire, and taste, CBS cancelled the show, and our little gang of funnymen and crazies was left out on the street, without any supervision. Ironically we went on to win that year's Emmy Award for Best Written Musical-Comedy-Variety series, accepting the gold statuette for a job we no longer had. Being Hot New Young Writers, we found other employment, kept in touch via comedy writer's yock-o-grams, and stayed in television until a few years later, when our lives changed. Steve got this white suit, stopped writing for others, went back to performing his own material (brilliantly and with great assurance), and found enormous personal success. I broke into feature film writing by co-authorizing JAWS, and later wrote a book about that experience.

By 1976, we were again Hot Stuff, and Steve and Bill McEuen, his friend and manager, formed the Aspen Film Society. David Picker, then one of the heads of Paramount Pictures, brought Aspen and Steve to that studio to create and star in two pictures and a short subject. The short was called THE ABSENT-MINDED WAITER, Steve starred in it, I directed it, and in 1978 it was nominated for an Academy Award in the live-action documentary short-subject category. I collaborated with Steve on his first feature film, which we called EASY MONEY. It wasn't so easy. David Picker left Paramount, the studio decided it didn't want to do EASY MONEY or any other Steve Martin picture. The Aspen Film Society and David Picker then got together with Universal Studios, where the film was ultimately made. EASY MONEY was revised by Steve and another old friend, Michael Elias, and Carl Reiner signed to direct. Carl worked on the picture with Steve, the title was changed to THE JERK, and the final, revised, last-draft shooting script, written by Steve Martin, Carl Gottlieb, and Michael Elias was filmed in Los Angeles from March 19th to May 17th, 1979.

MIDDLEGROUND

Movies are a linear form of entertainment; they unfold along the iron line of time in a series of sequential images. If that's too technical, consider this: unroll a movie, and you've got a strip of celluloid one and a half inches wide, and more than a mile and a half long. 1½″ by 105,000′ is linear, any way you look at it. Therefore, in a happy decision to let the book parallel the movie, we've adopted the same, linear sequential order: the pictures in the front of the book are of the beginning of the movie, the pictures at the back of the book are of the end of the movie, and the pages in between are the photos of the middle of the movie. What could be simpler? The text and captions were written to accommodate the pictorial elements, and out of a perverse sense of fun, certain liberties have been taken. Some captions and text do not describe anything in the movie, although they are absolutely faithful to the pictures they accompany, others are actual dialogue from the screenplay.

In this book, Steve dances, a Mad Sniper shoots at him, a Biker Carnival Girl seduces him, he meets his true love, he gets rich, he gets silly. These are pictures anyone can understand, perhaps even without seeing the movie. But THE JERK book aims at more complex texture, more erotic levels of interpretation, so it offers a variety of photo-explanations.

FOREGROUND

THE JERK takes place in a time resembling the Present, in a place that resembles America in the third quarter of the 20th century. Steve Martin plays Navin Johnson, a young man who one night realizes that his destiny lies somewhere outside the Mississippi Delta sharecropper's farm on which he has been raised. Navin goes out into the world to discover his roots, and along the way he discovers the joys of honest labor, the hazards of life in the city, the love of two very different women, and the experience of sudden, enormous wealth. Eventually Navin finds himself on the streets, a derelict. That Bum is the one who tells us his story, from start to finish. That Bum is THE JERK, and this is the book of pictures of the movie. We hope you enjoy it.

Carl Gottlieb
Hollywood, California
1979

The JERK

Navin Johnson's family celebrates his birthday at home with a sing-a-long.

Navin (standing on the porch) nods happily, out of sync as usual.

Here Navin conducts, using a kitchen
utensil as a baton.

His brother (the young man in the background) applauds Navin's newly acquired rhythm as his sister makes a hasty retreat.

15

Navin is hugged by his mother in joyous celebration of his departure from the old homestead. Why is the family so happy to see him go? Maybe the vintage aviator's helmet has something to do with it.

*This is a sensitive, pensive study of our hero.
That's obvious from the photograph. What isn't
evident is the salami sandwich under his hat,
which accounts for the high-domed bulge to
Navin's normally shaped head. His expression
is perplexed as he tries to remember if
there was a lot of mayonnaise on the
sandwich, and, if so, what will it
do to his hair.*

Navin arrives in a service station, gains
employment, and tries to qualify as a
modified sportsman formula junior (a
type of race car). The above photo shows
his arrival, the upper right shows his
unsuccessful attempt at converting
himself into a vehicle (his turning radius
was impaired by his inability to steer
with his feet). The bottom photo, right,
shows Navin as the handsome, romantic
leading man he really is. Just look at
that *face.*

Patriotism, Duty, Honor, Responsibility. Navin has his first job and is proud to be a stalwart pump-jockey, the backbone of the retail gas delivery system.

NOTE TO THOSE READERS UNDER 25

There was a time in American history when gas station attendants wore uniforms with ties, cleaned windshields, checked tires, oil, and batteries, gave away free dishes and road maps, and sold gas for 29.9 cents a gallon. That was during the same period when mail was delivered twice a day, New York City worked, and Hollywood made 300 new films a year. Can you guess the year?

(A) 1887 (B) 1906 (C) 1929 (D) 1950

That's right—1950. If you marked (D), give yourself a passing grade.

Dear Mom,
I got this great job in a gas station. I don't want to say just how much I'm getting, but let's just say it's a lot. I'm enclosing two dollars...

...it's a lot of fun working and Mr. Hartounian is really nice. He is teaching me how to be impatient. Well, I've got to go now. What do you think I do? ...Write letters all day? Your loving son,

Navin

24

Some Hoods and Low Riders are out cruising and stop at Hartounian's gas station. They are about to make trouble for Navin.

In order to more fully understand this picture, turn the book slowly clockwise (around to the right) until the figure of the man seems to be standing upright.

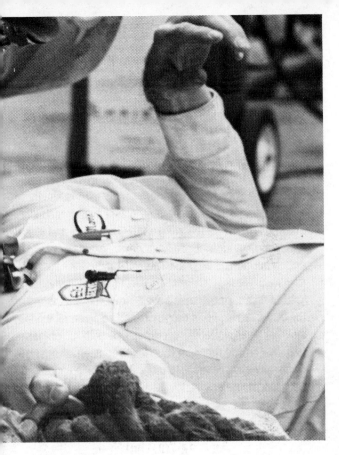

Study the photo carefully and you will see that it is a picture of Navin on his back under a car, just underneath the bumper and rear license plate. Now, turn the book counter clockwise (around to the left), until it is once again in the normal reading position.

You are now lined up to continue reading normally. Turn page.

A GREAT MOMENT IN SCIENCE

Navin Johnson, simple garage mechanic, works on "Opti-Grab"—a device that is destined to make his fortune and to change his life.

Simply described, the Opti-Grab diverts primary pressure from the nosepiece and hinges of conventional eyeglasses, and directs support to the sturdy bridge of the nose, via a welded-wire addition that fastens simply to any existing twin-lens pair of glasses or spectacles. Clearly, this is an idea whose time has come and is not a casual invention or dramatic device created simply to enrich our hero. The Opti-Grab was (and is) the result of painstaking research, and its use does not necessarily lead to disfiguring crossed-eyes. However, full testing of the Opti-Grab is still in progress, and commercial models may become available for street use without prescription. Watch for them at your local optician, drugstore, or novelty shop. They also may be on sale in your neighborhood theater.

OPTI-GRAB.

An Idea You Can See.

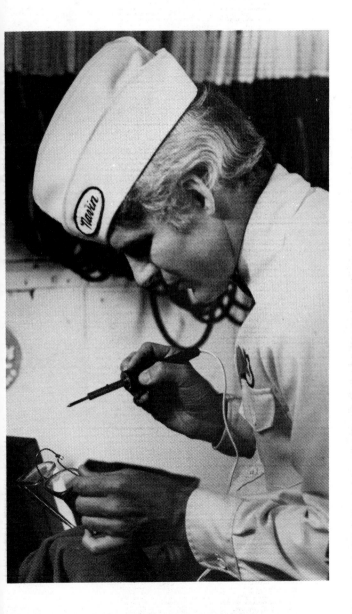

Stanley Fox, Promoter, is wearing the Opti-Grab, (Left), while Navin Johnson (Below) doubles over in reaction to the first appearance of his invention.

The Madman is a sniper determined to give Navin a hard time. Here he fastens a silencer to the barrel of what appears to be an M-16. Weapon buffs—is this possible? We know it's illegal.

?

**Can you guess what this madman is shooting at?
Some possible suggestions:**

- ☐ a gasoline station.

- ☐ a tall rabbit.

- ☐ a short giraffe.

- ☐ a _____ .

- ☐ a _____ .

Navin Johnson joins
C.F. Ferlinger's
Travelling Sideshow
and Carnival. Here he
is dressed for work.

I'LL GUESS YOUR

Weight WITHIN 3 LBS.

Occupation

WIN A

Navin is guessing age, weight, and
occupation on The Midway. His new friend
is Patty Bernstein who is an aggressive
carnival dare-devil.

I'LL
GUESS
YOUR

AGE
WITHIN 1 YR

HOME
STATE

Patty Bernstein's make-up and costume were specially designed (not just thrown together) for her carnival act, and to wear to the market or walk the dog.

Here Navin applauds Patty for her realistic impression of SUPERMAN.

43

CARNIVAL LIFE IS TOUGH

Navin (above) talks Patty into wearing a helmet for her famous "Riding Over a VW Backwards" stunt. She agrees, and is shown (right) ascending the hood end of the VW, in preparation for her leap backwards.

CARNIVAL LIFE IS BORING

Patty (below), in the midst of a seemingly difficult stunt, is totally ignored by the few passers-by on the Midway, only one of whom actually turns his head to watch, while walking in the opposite direction to get a corn-dog from the concession stand (not shown).

Right: Navin Johnson at his new job. His hat says "Engineer Fred." **Below:** Patty Bernstein seems to be in a pensive mood. Just out of sight of the camera, specially defanged wild dogs are attacking her feet, with comic results.

Navin meets his true love, Marie, who is taking care of little Billy for a friend.

LIFE IN A CARNIVAL
IS STILL BORING

Despite the fact that a man is caught with a roundhouse right to the stomach, nobody in the background seems to care. There's lots to see in a Carnival, and a fight between Patty and Navin has no attraction for these jaded fun-seekers.

LIFE IN A CARNIVAL IS ROUGH, PART II

Below: Patty gives Navin a rough time, based on her assumption that he has been seeing another woman (not shown, but you might've guessed, it's Marie).

TO MARIE

TWO WOMEN IN
NAVIN JOHNSON'S LIFE

Patty, (Above) whom we've already
described at some length, gets the
smaller picture, and Marie, Navin's True
Love (Right), gets the photo coverage
and billing to which she's entitled.

Left to right: Marie Kimball, a Sprig of
Brush, and Navin Johnson, who is
presenting the latter to the former as a

love-offering. Navin has fallen for Marie.
Their deepening involvement is further
illustrated on the following pages.

56

Navin and Marie have just concluded an intimate dinner, some tasty pizza-in-a-cup.

THEIR FIRST SCREEN KISS

Navin and Marie look deep into each
other's eyes (Above), and then (Right)
bring their lips together for the first
screen kiss. Well, perhaps not
actually together, but close.

Simultaneous self-expression; Navin and Marie sing the sixth tone of the scale together in a tender moment.

Honey, there's a question I'd like to pop but I've been afraid...that you might say no...But this seems like the right time and place...so here goes! Marie, will you marry me?

But, alas, Marie sends him a Dear Navin letter which he reads in the tub.

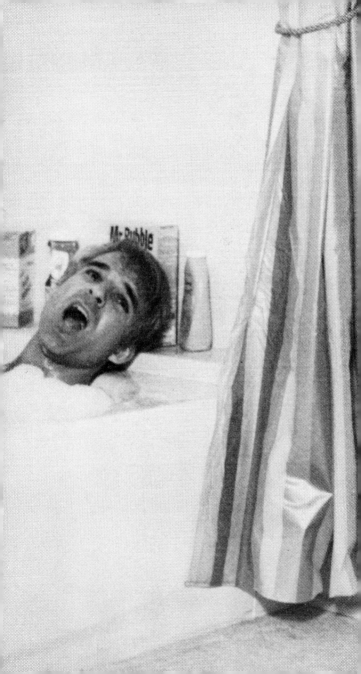

After reading Marie's wet letter,
Navin races out to find her.

You'd like her, Ma...Her name is Marie Kimball...
She's worth every pain I'll have to go through...And so,
Mom, with my faithful dog leading the way...I'm out
to become the man she desires. I'm only going to take
jobs that lead somewhere big.

Your loving son,
Navin

66

But fortune has been smiling on our struggling hero. For Stanley Fox, the facile entrepreneur, parlays Navin's humble invention into a business empire worth millions. The technical aspects of Opti-Grab are discussed earlier, on p. 28; the esthetic aspects are explored here by the models in the photographs that adorn the walls of Fox's office.

NOTHING WITHOUT LABOUR.

Money is the traditional reward for ingenuity and originality in the marketplace, according to the tenets of free-market capitalism. Find a need, create a desire, and people will find their way to your door, dollars in their fists, begging for a chance to buy whatever it is you've got they think they need.

Navin Johnson and Stanley Fox are part of this great tradition. Opti-Grab is an Idea whose time has come. The envelope in Stan Fox's hand in the bottom photograph at right, is Navin's "Cut," his share, the money he is owed, the dollars he has earned. From now on, his life is going to be different. Change is the unforeseen, inevitable camp follower to the glittering armies of the nouveaux riches. Capitalism, like Virtue, has its own rewards.

71

$ $ $ $ $

The face of a man who's life has changed. Notice how many teeth are showing. This is no ordinary smile. This is a real grin. And check the glasses—no ordinary spectacles with an Opti-Grab tacked on, these are custom butterfly-tinted shades, and when you look through them the world is colored like money—green, black, white, and lots of little images of Benjamin Franklin and Ulysses S. Grant floating in ovals just under where it says: "Federal Reserve Note." You look at the world that way, and your life will be different.

Harry Hartounian and his wife
Leonore get the news from Navin, via
postcard. From now on, it's spend,
spend, spend.

Navin and his ever-faithful dog, Shithead, resplendent in their new attire, pause before leaving Navin's shabby apartment to seek life's splendors...and Marie.

Below: Shithead, wearing sunglasses and a baseball cap, smokes a pipe as he waits for Navin in their new pink Mustang.

YOUNG INVENTOR
STRIKES IT RICH

said yesterday that
arnings had risen 20
rd $285.9 million, or
m $238.1 million, or
e comparable period
ochester-based com-
t sales in the period
) a record $2 billion
ast year.

benefited from a
x rate and increased
said Walter A. Fal-
chief executive, and
, president.
added, however, that
results in the fourt
ected to be adversel;
unfavorable econom
the United States''
ance of the year will :
of recent substantial
iaterials costs and hi'

78

Navin finds one of life's splendors.
Now for Marie.

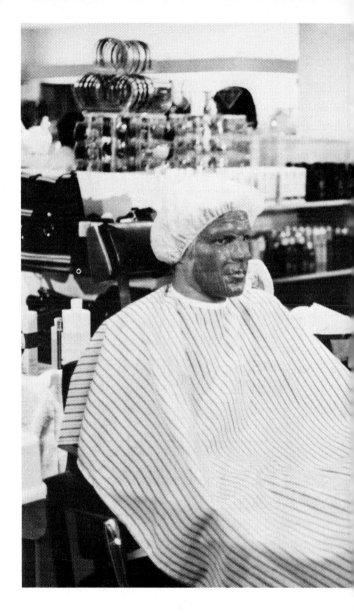

Navin finds Marie
working in a department
store in the men's
cosmetic section.
Unable to see his good
looks under a mask of
noxious clay, Marie
wonders about her old
friend from the Carnival.

Marie, about to peel off the
Mask-O-Derm is in for a surprise—Irving
has been replaced by—that's
right, NAVIN!

It's love
at last
for…

Best Wishes, Marie Kimball

SWEETHEARTS

your message here. Sincerely, Navin Johnson

Dear Mom,
Here's this month's check:
twenty thousand dollars. Things
are beginning to look up. But
the big news is, Marie and...I
were married! We couldn't wait.
We decided to get married that
night. Luckily, we found a
certified priest at the
"Hollywood View Apartments"
who could marry us.

Your loving son,
Navin

Marie's garage apartment is home for the Newlyweds. At right, Marie and Navin are playing house in the kitchen, tippy-toeing so as not to awaken Hobart and Hester, the English Butler and Maid, who are asleep on a single bed in the living room.

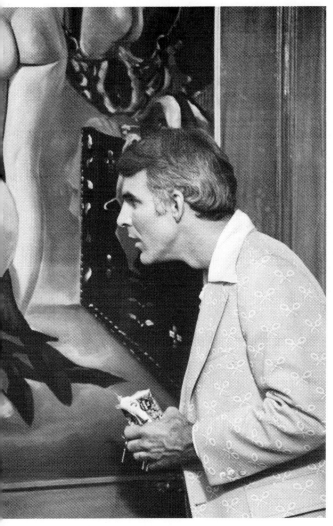

Navin and Marie consult a real estate
agent, who shows them a house complete
with paintings. This art has Navin
crushing his box of Cracker Jacks.

A NOTE ON CRACKER JACKS

The box Steve is holding in both photos (Above, right) is good old Cracker Jacks, the kind you get at the zoo, or the ballgame. They have little prizes inside, usually a tiny paper book, a plastic toy or novelty. There's one important thing to know about Cracker Jacks: the fresh boxes rattle when you shake them, the stale ones don't—the carmel coating has stuck all the little Cracker Jacks together. They're still good to eat, but they're not individual anymore. And does anyone know if there's still as many peanuts in the boxes as there used to be?

95

RICH!

Navin stands smiling in the driveway of his new home, which the staff (right) seems to think is more appropriate to their station.

Navin in bed. Is this the life, or is this the life?

Dear Mom,
Marie and I are getting along swell. I've got
a lot to learn. What with signing checks,
learning about credits and debentures,
certificates of deposit...you have to be
careful....Enclosed is this week's check.

Your loving son,
Navin

The new Navin displays a depth of
attitude and a rugged handsomeness.
So does Marie.

Navin, already rich beyond his wildest imaginings, is approached by Con Men with nefarious schemes. They don't know what they're getting into, but neither does Navin.

Naturally, the family manse has a fabulous, private movie screening room. Do Navin and Marie show "JAWS" or "LA CAGE AUX FOLLES"?
You bet they don't. What they screen is this grainy, black and white, documentary style film that is brought to Navin by Carlos Las Vegas de Cordoba.

CAT JUGGLING, MEXICAN STYLE

was filmed under impossible conditions and smuggled out of the country. The first footage ever shot of this new sport is unreeled on the next few pages. When the flying pussycats are finished, they will be returned to the basket, which is being held by "The Juggler" on the opposite page.

Kittens airborne,
no wires.
No gimmicks.
True Juggling.

Above: An exciting moment as the little kitties whiz through the air in furry circles, their mews and meows drowned out by the roars of the appreciative crowd. It is reported that there is spirited wagering on the sidelines as to how many circuits a cat will complete before it's dropped, how high they'll go, and the "Quinella," in which a courageous bettor can win enormous pay-offs by successfully predicting the five directions five cats will run when dropped simultaneously to the floor.

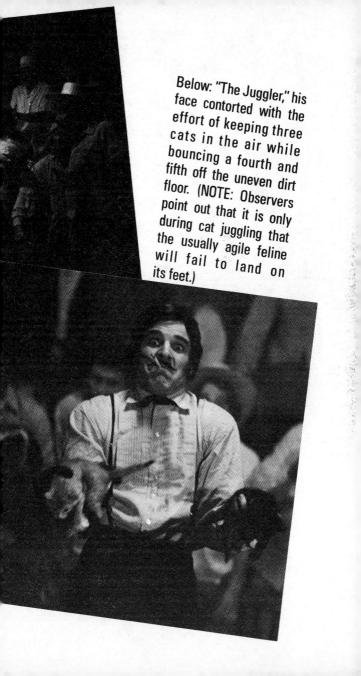

Below: "The Juggler," his face contorted with the effort of keeping three cats in the air while bouncing a fourth and fifth off the uneven dirt floor. (NOTE: Observers point out that it is only during cat juggling that the usually agile feline will fail to land on its feet.)

Navin and Marie are living it up, dining out at a French restaurant. Service is slow, which explains their bored expressions and the behavior of the diner in the center background, who is eating his thumb and forefinger while waiting for his appetizer. At right, Navin is taking exception to the escargot on Marie's plate, while The Waiter stands by in dismay.

Above: Navin and Marie get up to kiss,
but the weight of the gold chains around
his neck (right) puts him into the soup.

...And, Mom, I love to write and tell you all about what Marie and I are up to. Our days are so full—and so are our nights which are spent in our very own basement disco....

We dance the night away, Mom...

Marie: Is this what we really want?

Navin: Sure!

It's such fun. Marie and I are really drinking a lot. It's great! We get wobbly and real funny. You'd be so proud of us. Enclosed is your regular check.

Your loving son,
Navin

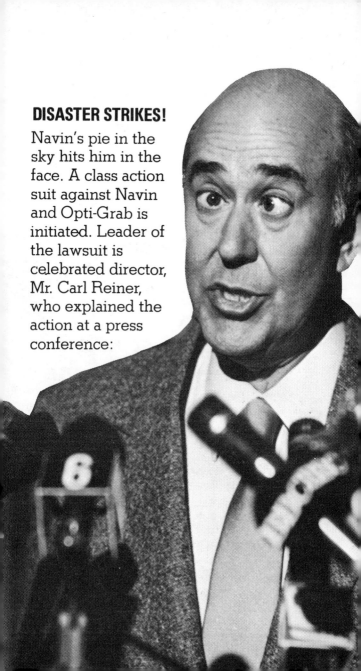

DISASTER STRIKES!

Navin's pie in the sky hits him in the face. A class action suit against Navin and Opti-Grab is initiated. Leader of the lawsuit is celebrated director, Mr. Carl Reiner, who explained the action at a press conference:

When Opti-Grab came out, I thought it was the greatest thing ever, and I bought a pair. And this is the result…That little handle is like a magnet; your eyes are constantly drawn to it, and you end up cock-eyed. And as a director I am constantly using my eyes and the Opti-Grab device has caused irreparable harm to my career.

Now Navin is in deep trouble. Facing the
loss of his new-found wealth, he appeals
to the judge and jury and confronts his
accusers—among them (and their leader)
his own director, Carl Reiner, playing Carl
Reiner, the Director. Marie watches,
knowing all is lost and that the party's
really over.

Navin loses everything. He's flat broke.

NAVIN IN DISTRESS: TWO VIEWS.

Left; Profile, walking.
Below: Full front view, standing.

Navin leaves Marie, taking with him a few belongings from their home.

Navin, deprived of money, fame, and fortune, turns to the bottle, and is shown here draining life's bitter dregs. A tasty potation of wormwood and gall, cheap muscatel and spoiled vanilla extract, it is the street-person's favorite brew, the bagman's Beaujolais.

"Oooh-Wheee," Navin seems to be saying as he savors the aftertaste of the drink described above. His street companions have no reaction; they're nursing their own drinks, or napping off the effects of earlier swallows.

Navin, on the edge of despair, is discovered by his family, who welcome him back with open arms. Navin is clutching a little Thermos bottle in his right arm.

And Navin is reminded that there's no place like

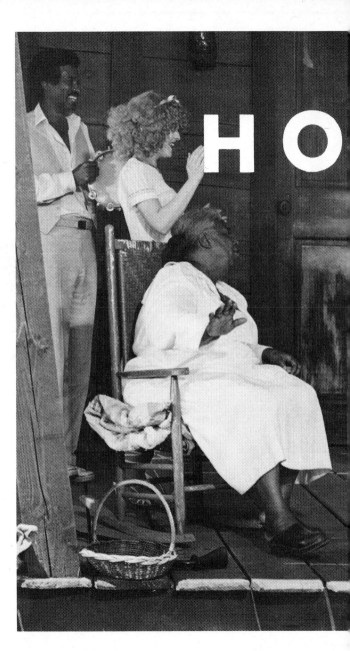

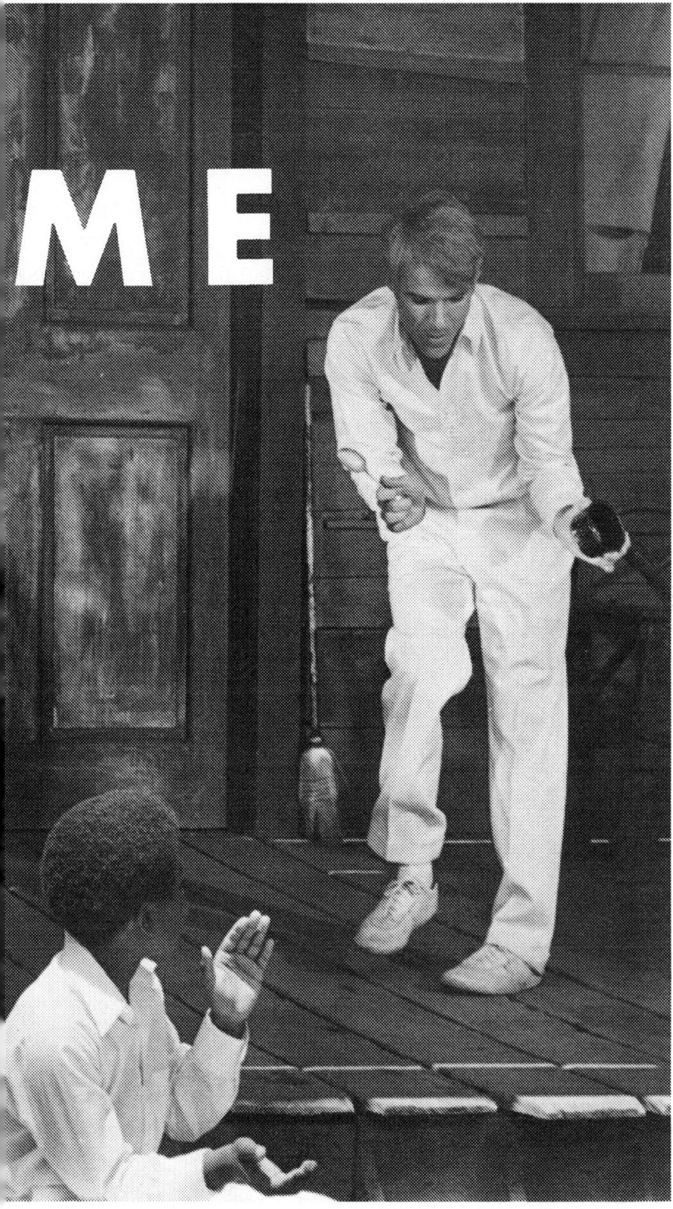
ME

And so, as in all good fairy tales, our

ero and heroine live happily ever after. Or do they? We'll have to wait for the sequel—THE JERK 2 (or maybe TWO JERKS)—to find out....

Now how about a round of applause for all the people who brought you THE JERK....

UNIVERSAL PICTURES PRESENTS

**AN ASPEN FILM SOCIETY
WILLIAM E. McEUEN-DAVID V. PICKER
PRESENTATION**

A CARL REINER FILM

STEVE MARTIN

in

THE JERK

Directed by CARL REINER
Produced by DAVID V. PICKER and WILLIAM E. McEUEN
Screenplay by STEVE MARTIN,
CARL GOTTLIEB, MICHAEL ELIAS
Based on a story by STEVE MARTIN & CARL GOTTLIEB

Cast of Characters

Navin	STEVE MARTIN
Marie	BERNADETTE PETERS
Patty Bernstein	CATLIN ADAMS
Mother	MABEL KING
Father	RICHARD WARD
Taj	DICK ANTHONY WILLIAMS
Stan Fox	BILL MACY
Madman	M. EMMET WALSH
Frosty	DICK O'NEILL
Hobart	MAURICE EVANS
Hester	HELENA CARROLL
Elvira	REN WOOD
Punk #1	PEPE SERNA
Blues Singer	SONNY TERRY
Blues Singer	BROWNIE McGEE
Harry Hartounian	JACKIE MASON
Bank Manager	DAVID LANDSBERG
Father De Cordoba	DOMINGO AMBRIZ
Grandma Johnson	FRANCES E. WILLIAMS
Cleotis Johnson	LYDIA McGHEE
Satch Johnson	NIKO DENISE HOLMES

Pierre Johnson	SHAWN HARRIS
Leroy Johnson	NILES HARRIS
Lisa Johnson	SUSAN DENISE HARRISON
Iron Balls McGinty	CARL GOTTLIEB
Con Man	RICHARD FORONJY
Con Man	LENNY MONTANA
Con Man	GENE LEBELL
Con Man	FRED LERNER
Announcer	CLETE ROBERTS
Fireman	DOUGLAS S. CLOSE
Mrs. Hartounian	SHARON JOHANSEN
Punk	TRINIDAD SILVA
Bride	ALSTON AHERN
Father of Bride	LAWRENCE GREEN
Stunts	DEBBIE EVANS
Carnival Rube	KEN MAGEE
Tourist	TOM J. DELANEY
Irving	ALFRED DENNIS
Farm Boy	MARC LOGE
Billy	JON LEICHTER
Tillie	LILLIAN ADAMS
Irving	ALFRED DENNIS
Cat Juggler	PIG EYE JACKSON
Voodoo Dancer	JOE LYNN
French Waiter	MAURICE MARSAC
Man in Garden	JERRY G. VELASCO
Disco Party	KIMBERLY CAMERON
	ELIZABETH MACEY
	RICHIE REINER
	DANIEL TREVOR
Carl Reiner, The Celebrity	HIMSELF

Director of Photography	VICTOR J. KEMPER, A.S.C.
Film Editor	BUD MOLIN
Also Edited by	RON SPANG
Music Composed and Conducted by	JACK ELLIOTT
Associate Producer	PETER MACGREGOR-SCOTT
Production Designer	JACK T. COLLIS
Costume Designer	THEADORA VAN RUNKLE
Production Manager	PETER MACGREGOR-SCOTT
First Assistant Director	NEWTON ARNOLD
Second Assistant Director	ED MILKOVICH
Location Manager	DOW GRIFFITH
Camera Operator	ROBERT THOMAS
Assistant Cameraman	ROBERT MARTA
Special Effects	HENRY MILLAR
Stills	STEPHEN VAUGHAN
Stunt Coordinator	CONRAD PALMISANO
Casting by	PENNY PERRY
	GINO HAVENS
Set Director	JOE HUBBARD
Set Decorations	RICHARD GODDARD
Sound	CHARLES M. WILBORN
Sound Rerecording	WILLIAM L. McCAUGHEY
	HOPPY MEHTERIAN
	EDDIE NELSON
Sound Effects Editors	GORDON DANIEL
	GIL MARCHANT
	TONY POLK
	KEITH STAFFORD
Music Director	MILTON LUSTIG
Loop Dialogue Editor	MARVIN I. KOSBERG
Make-Up	DEL ACEVEDO
Hair Stylist	BARBARA LORENZ
Costume Supervisors	MICHAEL J. HARTE
	APRIL FERRY
Script Supervisor	MARSHAL WOLINS
Property Master	DENNIS PARRISH
Gaffer	EARL GILBERT